Zach Gets Frustrated

William Mulcahy

illustrated by
Darren McKee

free spirit
PUBLISHING®

Library of Congress Cataloging-in-Publication Data
Mulcahy, William.
  Zach gets frustrated / William Mulcahy ; illustrated by Darren McKee.
    p. cm. — (Zach rules series)
  ISBN 978-1-57542-390-6 — ISBN 978-1-57542-669-3 (ebook) 1. Frustration—Juvenile literature. I. McKee, Darren II. Title.
  BF723.F7M85 2012
  152.4'7—dc23

                                                                                    2011039185

eBook ISBN: 978-1-57542-669-3

Reading Level Grades 2 & 3; Interest Level Ages 5–8;
Fountas & Pinnell Guided Reading Level M

Edited by Eric Braun
Cover and interior design by Tasha Kenyon

10 9 8 7 6 5 4 3 2 1
Printed in the United States of America
B10950212

Free Spirit Publishing Inc.
Minneapolis, MN
(612) 338-2068
help4kids@freespirit.com
www.freespirit.com

Dedication

To Liam, Luke, and Jack:
Enjoy the moment

Acknowledgments

Deep gratitude to all of those who have entrusted me with their care and well-being; I am deeply honored to be your therapist. A special thanks to my colleagues at Family Service of Waukesha and Carrie and Melissa at Stillwaters. Lastly, to the wow-moment in Aunt Kelly's kitchen with Kristen, Ryan, and Meghan: Thanks for helping out. You rock.

Zach lifted his kite and ran across the beach. He hoped this time the breeze would catch it. But like the other times he'd tried, the kite just fluttered and dived into the sand.

"Stupid kite," Zach said. Since the day began, it seemed like nothing was going his way. And now his kite wouldn't fly.

Zach tried to relax. But it's hard to calm down when your breath is heavy and you feel like screaming.

"When are we going home?" he asked his dad.

"What's the matter?" Dad asked. "You love the beach."

"Everything's going wrong today," Zach said. "Especially this dumb kite that doesn't even fly."

Dad curled his toes into the soft sand. "You sound pretty frustrated."

"So, can we go home or what?" Zach asked.

"Well, your brothers and I are having a good time," Dad said. "What if I showed you a way to help yourself feel better so you can enjoy yourself, too? Then we can all stay."

"I can't enjoy myself. This is worse than the day I threw up at school."

5

"Let's give it a try," Dad said. "There are three steps I follow that help me handle my frustration. The first step is to **name it.**" He wrote that in the sand by a corner of the kite.

1. name it

"Ha!" Zach said. "I already **have** a name for it: Stupid, stinking, idiotic, no-fun kite."

Zach's dad just gave him a funny look.

1.
name it

"All right," Zach said. "What do you mean?"

"Frustration is what we feel when things don't go the way we want them to," his dad said. "It's important to talk about the thing that frustrates you. That's why you name it: You say in words what the problem is."

"Do you ever get frustrated?" Zach asked.

"Oh, yeah. Remember last week when I had so much trouble fixing Alex's bike chain?"

1. name it

"You pinched your finger and you got grease on your shirt. You were pretty mad."

"Pretty **frustrated**," Dad said. "So what made *you* frustrated?"

Zach thought. "I guess I'm frustrated because I can't fly this kite."

2. tame it

"Okay," Dad said. "Now, the second step is to **tame it.** That means using your chill skills to help your mind and body relax. You can take deep breaths, count slowly to ten, or concentrate on a nice sound like ocean waves."

Dad said, "Here's one I really like. I squeeze my face and hands real tight for a few seconds and then let go.

"When you let that tension go, you get more relaxed than you were before. Let me show you."

1. name it

2. tame it

Zach wasn't in the mood to scrunch up his face and hands. But his dad had taught him some other chill skills. The trick was to practice one or two that you liked so you'd remember them easily.

Meditate

Stretch

Picture something you love

Zach closed his eyes and listened to the waves crashing onto the beach.

He breathed in slowly through his nose and out through his mouth. Then he did it again: in through the nose, out through the mouth.

He felt his body loosening up.

"Good," Dad said. "Now you're ready for the last step: **reframe it.**"

"Reframe it?" Zach asked.

"It means you look at the problem in a new way. When the kite wouldn't fly, I bet you said lots of negative things in your head. I bet you've been thinking crabby thoughts all day."

Zach realized his dad was right. A voice in his head had been saying this was the worst day in the history of the world—and other grumpy things. He thought about those grumpy thoughts again.

His best friend Sonya chose to go to the theme park with another friend instead of coming to the beach with Zach.

He dropped his toothbrush in the toilet.

And he stepped on the edge of the litter box and spilled it all over the floor—and his foot.

"See, your thoughts affect your feelings," Dad said. "When you **think** things are bad, then you **feel** bad. Guess what can happen when you change—or reframe—those bad thoughts into good ones?"

"What's the point?" Zach said. "Bad stuff still happened to me. If I had a magic wand, I'd make everything go the way I want!"

"You can't change what happened to you," Dad said. "But you can change what you **think** about what happened. For example, when Sonya said she couldn't come, you thought, 'Nobody likes me.' Instead, try thinking, 'Sonya is a good friend. I will see her soon.'"

Zach thought about what his dad said. And he remembered that he and Sonya had a soccer game tomorrow, which was always fun. Surprisingly, he did feel a little better. So he thought about that voice in his head that said this was the worst day ever. He knew it wasn't really true, so he changed his thought.

Zach said, "This kite won't fly, but the beach is awesome. I love jumping in the waves." He looked out at the people splashing in the water.

"How do you feel?" asked Dad.

"Pretty good, I guess. But I'll never remember all these steps."

"Check this out," Dad said, tracing the kite. "A triangle has three points, right?" He pointed to the corners. "Name it, tame it, reframe it. We'll call this the frustration triangle."

The triangle was a good idea. Zach closed his eyes and practiced picturing the triangle with the words at each corner.

3. reframe it

2. tame it

When he saw **"name it,"** he'd say why he was frustrated.

1. name it

2. tame it

3. reframe it

When he saw **"tame it,"** he'd do deep breathing or another chill skill.

And when he saw **"reframe it,"** he'd change his negative thoughts to positive ones.

For now, he wanted to enjoy the beach, so he ran out into the waves to swim. When he got out of the water, maybe he'd try that kite again.

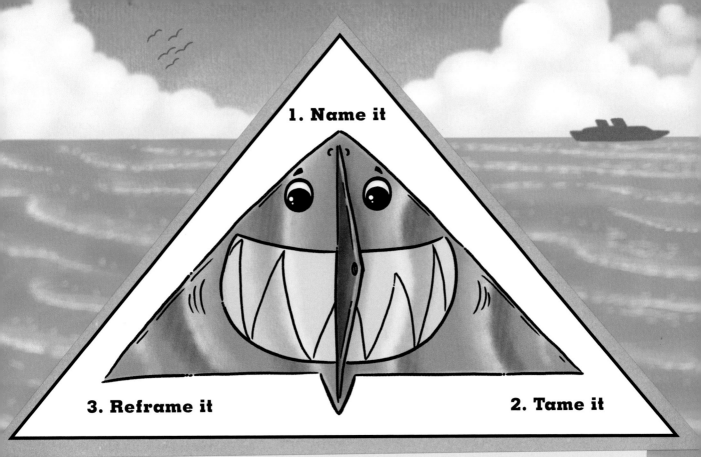

1. Name it

3. Reframe it

2. Tame it

When Zach uses the frustration triangle, he handles his frustration in a healthy way instead of letting it get the best of him.

For help with your frustration, you can use Zach's frustration triangle. Just like Zach, you can name it, tame it, and reframe it, to help yourself feel better when things aren't going your way.

Helping Children Handle Frustration

As young children grow up, they continually encounter new tasks to accomplish and grow from—and also to become frustrated by. In many instances, children's success depends on their ability to endure or overcome frustration—the feeling we get when we can't do what we are trying to do or we can't solve a problem facing us. Showing children how to cope with frustration in a way that puts them in charge of their thoughts and feelings not only helps them accomplish particular tasks, it helps prepare them for a lifetime of success.

The frustration triangle is a three-step process that helps kids develop the inner awareness and control they need to endure and manage frustration. While each of the three steps is important on its own, together they create a gentle but powerful tool to manage emotions.

The frustration triangle is most successful when adults and children are partners in learning about and practicing the three steps. Unfortunately, adults often misunderstand frustration; or worse, they take it personally as an affront to their parenting skills. Keep in mind that frustration is a naturally occurring emotion that all people experience. Approach frustrated children with understanding and compassion. Modeling understanding and compassion will also help children treat themselves that way while frustrated.

The frustration triangle has the power to

- build confidence
- increase a sense of peace and calmness
- decrease the likelihood of the fight-or-flight response in the brain
- increase the likelihood of successfully dealing with frustration and other difficult emotions in the future
- lift feelings of sadness and anxiety
- enhance relationships

Important: The frustration triangle is not about stuffing emotions. Help children understand that frustration is a natural emotion and that emotions are not bad or good. It's what they do with their emotions that matters. Ideally, children can feel, identify, and deal with their emotions in a healthy way.

If children are constantly frustrated or often intensely frustrated, seek professional help.

Here is more information about the three parts of the frustration triangle. With practice, most children will be able to move fluidly from step 1 (name it) to step 2 (tame it) to step 3 (reframe it).

1. **Name it.** In this step, children make themselves aware of what is causing their frustration. This may sound overly simple or obvious, but naming the source of frustration increases people's awareness of their emotional state. This increased awareness puts them in a stronger position to cope with their emotion. With coaching and practice, most children are able to identify their emotions very accurately, including frustration.

2. **Tame it.** Help children move out of their automatic thoughts and into the present moment by using relaxation skills (what are referred to in this story as "chill skills"). Using these skills helps the mind let go of the frustration. These skills may include slow deep breathing, counting to ten, progressive relaxation, spending time in nature, prayer, meditation, listening to music, playing, and mindfulness practices (focusing on the senses).

3. **Reframe it.** At first, teach children to be specific in reframing frustrating situations. For instance, "This kite won't fly, but the beach is awesome. I love jumping in the waves." As children become more efficient, they often learn to reframe frustration with a simple "Everything's okay" or "This too will pass."

A few other tips:

- Teach children the frustration triangle before it is needed, when frustration isn't high, so they know what to expect. Let them know that you believe they can handle their frustration.
- Encourage children to develop their own ways to name it, tame it, and reframe it. As long as they are following the basic structure, let them be playful and use their imagination.
- Use the frustration triangle yourself. You might be surprised at how helpful it can be!
- Encourage kids not to be too hard on themselves. Everyone gets frustrated.

You can't change what happens to your children, but you can equip them to handle frustration more effectively. Providing them with positive coaching and tools such as the frustration triangle helps them change the way they react to frustration, from being hijacked emotionally to thinking clearly and acting skillfully.

Download a printable copy of the frustration triangle at www.freespirit.com/Frustration.

William Mulcahy is a licensed professional counselor, psychotherapist, and supervisor of the Cooperative Parenting Center at Family Service of Waukesha, Wisconsin. He has served as a consultant at Stillwaters Cancer Support Center in Wisconsin, specializing in grief and cancer-related issues, and he has worked with children with special needs. Bill's short stories have appeared in several publications. The Zach Rules books are his first books for children, merging his passions for good storytelling and providing counseling-like tools to help children live healthier, happier lives. Bill lives in Summit, Wisconsin, with his three sons, who played their own role in the creation of the Zach Rules series. His website is wmulcahy.com.

Darren McKee has illustrated books for many publishers over his 20-year career. When not working, he spends his time riding his bike, reading, drawing, and traveling. He lives in Dallas, Texas, with his wife Debbie.

More Great Books from Free Spirit

Zach Apologizes
by William Mulcahy, illustrated by Darren McKee

When Zach shoves his little brother to the floor, he knows he did something wrong. Even so, it's hard to apologize—especially when Alex kind of deserved it! Like any seven-year-old, Zach tries to ignore the problem, but finally, with his mom's help, he learns the four steps to apologizing: 1) say what you did, 2) tell how it made the other person feel, 3) say what you could have done instead, 4) make it up to the person. The apology strategy is presented as the "four-square" apology, which is illustrated with a step in each square. Kids will easily understand and remember this tool.
32 pp., illust., 4-color, H/C, 8" x 8". Ages 5–8.

Our Emotions and Behavior Series
by Sue Graves, illustrated by Desideria Guicciardini

Small children have big feelings. The Our Emotions and Behavior series uses cheerful, brightly illustrated stories to help kids understand how their emotions and actions are related—and how they can learn to manage both. Follow along as Noah, Ben, Nora, and their friends discover ways to deal with fears, sadness, rules, and sharing. At the end of each book, a two-page series of pictures invites kids to tell a story in their own words. A special section for adults suggests discussion questions and ideas for guiding children to talk about their feelings. *Each book: 32 pp., illust., 4-color, H/C, 7¾" x 9½". Ages 4–8.*

Interested in purchasing multiple quantities? Contact edsales@freespirit.com
or call 1.800.735.7323 and ask for Education Sales.

Many Free Spirit authors are available for speaking engagements, workshops, and keynotes.
Contact speakers@freespirit.com or call 1.800.735.7323.

For pricing information, to place an order, or to request a free catalog, contact:

free spirit PUBLISHING ®

217 Fifth Avenue North • Suite 200 • Minneapolis, MN 55401-1299
toll-free 800.735.7323 • local 612.338.2068 • fax 612.337.5050
help4kids@freespirit.com • www.freespirit.com

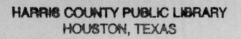